NICO

EYE CANDY INK BOOK 5

SHAW HART

BLURB

Nico Miller is the quiet silent type. With ten years experience, he's probably the best artist at the shop. He's a giant at 6'8" and built like a linebacker with tattoos covering his neck and torso. Most people are a little afraid of him when they first meet him but it doesn't take long to see that while he might look scary, with his almost permanent frown, tattoos, and size, he was actually a giant teddy bear.

He doesn't really care what people think about him, preferring to spend his time alone with his drawing pad. That is until he meets Edie West. She's smart, successful, driven, and the most beautiful thing that he's ever seen.

Most of the time he can't wait for people to leave but one encounter with Edie and he doesn't want to let her go. Will he be able to convince her that settling down with him doesn't mean settling?

ico

"I'M NOT SAYING that we need a bigger place, just a new bed," Indie says as Mischa holds the front door open for her.

We're about to open and she must be dropping him off. I ignore them as I lean back in my chair and continue to sketch on my pad. I have a "celebrity" client coming in later today and I'm going to need to relax and destress before he gets here.

I hate high profile clients. They never seem to want a tattoo because they want it. It's always more of a publicity thing, something for them to put online and show off. Plus, they always act so entitled, demanding that I pose for selfies with them and shit. I shudder just thinking about it.

"What's wrong with my bed?" Mischa asks as he comes over and plops down next to me.

He leans over, checking out my sketch and lets out a whistle.

"It's not comfortable," Indie says as she walks over to say hello to Sam and then comes and takes the seat on the other side of me. I briefly wonder if I'm being punished for something as they continue to argue across me.

"We need something that's not so soft," Indie says.

"I like soft, especially when we-" I don't wait to hear what he's about to say next, just slam my sketchpad shut and get the hell out of there.

Mischa's chuckling is cut off and I look back to see Indie smack him in the arm. I head into the back and into my room so that I don't have to watch Indie and Mischa say goodbye. Sam nods at me as I pass her and I hear the front door open and Zeke call out a hello. I hear the gate open and I know that he'll be stopping in my room soon.

He knocks on the doorframe and I notice that he seems distracted as he looks around the space.

"You all set for that VIP this afternoon?" He asks and I try to bite back my groan.

"Yeah," I mumble, pulling out my desk chair.

He grins at me before he leaves to go to his office and I know that he knows that I'm dreading it. I've been working for Zeke for close to a decade. I trained under him when I was first starting out. I was sixteen and he had just opened Eye Candy Ink. I lived in Pittsburgh all of my life and Eye Candy Ink was the first tattoo shop to open close to where I lived with my parents. Usually, they were further downtown, in the rougher area of the city.

I had always been good at art and something about tattoos always fascinated me. Maybe it was childhood rebellion but either way it worked out. I apprenticed under Zeke for two and a half years before he hired me on full time. I think maybe my parents were a little disappointed but they always tried to be supportive.

My parents are both psychologists, with a joint practice only a few blocks away from Eye Candy Ink. I should probably be the most well-adjusted person with parents who do what mine do, but that's not the case. I've always been big for my size and towering over my classmates and peers made me self-conscious and shy. I had always been quiet and more of an introvert and I know my parents worried about me but honestly, them psychoanalyzing me all of the time probably did more damage than good. I learned to only speak when I had to and to be very clear, very realistic, when I spoke.

I get my looks from my parents. They both have dark brown hair, but theirs always looks put together, neatly trimmed and pinned back. Mine is perpetually too long and gives me a shaggy, surfer kind of look. I have the same hazel eyes as my mother, with the same green ring around the pupil. My height is all from my dad. He's tall, although at 6'8", I'm still an inch taller than him. I'm big, built like a linebacker and most of my body is covered in tattoos. I know that most people tend to be afraid of me, especially when they first see me. Luckily, I don't care what most people think.

The shop opens a few minutes later and I get lost in my work, drowning out the buzz from the tattoo machines and the rock music that Mischa is blaring from his room and I just create. I get lost in my art and when I look up a few hours later, my eyes lock on a curvy goddess.

Brown hair falls in gentle waves around her heart shaped face. She flashes a wide smile my way, showing off a row of straight white teeth and I'm pretty sure my jaw drops. Her navy blue eyes twinkle and she twists her body to the side, showing off her voluptuous body. She's wearing a pair of dark blue dress slacks and a pastel striped blouse and I think seeing that kind of attire in the shop might be a first. My finger clench but I'm not sure if I want to reach for her curvy hips or for my drawing pencils and pad.

"Hi, I'm Edie. You must be Nico," the curvy goddess says, gifting me with a smile and I just about swallow my tongue.

This girl is mine.

For a second, I wonder if I'm dreaming, but then Pascal Gagne steps up next to her and I realize that it's not a dream. It's a nightmare.

I try to force a smile as I stand to welcome my VIP client.

2

E die

I'M NOT EVEN sure why I need to be here. Pascal Gagne, my client tonight, already had me translate the design that he wanted and we already went over the price and everything else. Pascal is the son of some rich Frenchman. His dad is a successful businessman who owns a few wineries. His son is a fuckboy. He prefers to party instead of work and with his dad's bank account he can get away with it. He's an annoyance and I can't wait to be done with him. If I didn't need the money then I would have left a long time ago, but I do, so instead I'm sitting here. At least the view isn't bad.

I shift in the chair, tucked away in the corner of the room and I don't even need to look to know that Nico's eyes are on me. The giant man seems to notice everything. I brush back my hair and his eyes are on me, I set my purse down and he watches me, I shift, breathe, blink, and I swear it's like he's cataloging it all.

I've been watching him too.

It's hard not to. The guy is huge and watching him work is fascinating. I never realized how loud a tattoo shop is but the noise from the tattoo machines and various music playing in each room makes it hard to hear. I get the feeling that Nico would rather not talk and it means less work for me so whatever.

I was a little scared of the guy when we first came in. He's the size of a brick building and when he didn't smile when we did introductions, it had caused a tiny spark of alarm. The more time I spent in this room with him though, the more I realized that that seemed to just be him.

The front receptionist girl had stopped by a couple of minutes ago to say goodbye and I had relaxed more when he had immediately asked her who was walking her to her car. She had rolled her eyes and said Atlas and I got the feeling that he was always looking out for her like that.

He's been patient with Pascal too. The pretentious asshole has whined and winced his way through the last three hours but Nico has been nothing but kind. He's offered him breaks and water and Pascal has taken everyone so the small tattoo that should have taken an hour, hour and a half tops, is now nearing three and a half hours.

I want nothing more than to leave and head back to the hotel. I had planned on ordering some room service but at this rate, the hotel kitchen was going to be closed by the time that I made it back there. Looks like it will be another night of Taco Bell, I think with a sigh and I notice Nico's eyes flick over to me.

After one more small break, the tattoo is done and I

think we all let out a big breath of relief as Nico starts to bandage him up. I watch his big hands as they smear on some ointment and then he grabs the bandages from his desk. Before he can wrap his arm though, Pascal turns to me.

"Qu'en penses-tu, Edie?"

What do you think, Edie?

"Cela semble bon, Monsieur Gagne," I reply, trying to remind him that this is a professional relationship. He's been hitting on me for most of the last four days and I am so ready for this job to be over.

"Dites au grand homme qu'il y a une fête dans ma chambre d'hôtel ce soir. Ça va faire rage. Il devrait venir le vérifier. Vous aussi, joues douces."

Tell the big man that there's a party at my hotel room tonight. It's going to be raging. He should come check it out. You too, sweet cheeks.

My teeth grit when he calls me sweet cheeks and I look over to Nico but his face is a blank mask as he tapes up the bandage on his arm.

"Vous devriez planifier votre heure avec moi maintenant, joues douces. Je ne peux pas promettre que je ne serai pas trop occupée avec d'autres filles à la fête."

You should schedule your hour with me now, sweet cheeks. I can't promise that I won't get too busy with other girls at the party.

He gestures to his dick when he says I should schedule my hour and I want to roll my eyes and say I assume he meant five minutes but I bite my tongue. Just a few more hours and I'll never have to see this prick again.

To my utter surprise and I think to Pascal's shock, Nico speaks up.

"Ce n'est pas comme ça que tu parles à une dame."

That's not how you speak to a lady.

My whole body warms as he sticks up to me and my thighs grow damp, listening to him speak fluent French in that deep voice of his. I clench my thighs tighter together and I swear I see Nico's lip quirk up at the motion.

3

Nico

THE FRENCH ASSHOLE shoves some money at me as he jerks off of the tattoo table and heads toward the front door. I can hear him on his phone, calling his car to pull around up front and making plans for his raging party tonight. I eye Edie, as she collects her purse and stands from the chair.

"Sorry about him," she murmurs but she doesn't need to apologize for some asshole's behavior so I don't say anything back.

"Do you have a ride?" I ask as I clean up my desk and put my equipment away.

"He was it, but I can call an Uber."

"I'll drive you," I tell her as I push my desk chair in and throw the disinfectant wipes in the trash.

"Oh, um, thank you," she says after a minute and I smile slightly, glad that I won't have to argue with her.

I make sure the shop is closed up and everything is put away before I lead her out the front door, setting the security alarm and locking the front door before I lead her up a block and over to my truck.

"Have you lived here long?" She asks as I open the passenger door for her.

"All my life."

I close the door after her and then climb behind the wheel. My old truck rumbles to life and I pull out of the parking spot.

"Which hotel are you staying at?"

"The Fairmont. On Market Street."

I nod and turn out of the lot, heading north toward downtown. Traffic isn't bad and I know that it will only take about fifteen minutes to get there. I don't normally enjoy being around a lot of people but there's something about Edie that I don't mind.

After we pass the third fast food place and I see how Edie practically drools against the window as she watches them go by in the window, I turn into the drive of a local burger place.

"Burgers and fries alright?" I ask and she nods back right away.

We drive through and order our food and I pull out my wallet, handing the cashier some bills and passing the greasy bag to Edie.

"Thanks for dinner. I was starving," she says as she unwraps one burger and passes it to me before she pulls out her own.

I nod as we both bite into our dinner. She polishes hers off in a matter of minutes and I tell her I don't want any of my fries. She happily digs into the bag, popping a few golden French fries in her mouth.

"How did you get into being an interpreter?" I ask after a beat.

She finishes chewing her mouthful, taking a big drink from her chocolate milkshake before she answers me.

"My mom worked for the state department so we moved around quite a bit when I was growing up. I was young enough and I picked up the languages easily. Over the years, I just kept up with them and then I went to college to get my degrees in them and interpreting was the next logical step."

I can hear the respect and love in her voice when she talks about her mom and I know she must look up to her.

"What about your dad?"

"I never met him. It was a one-night stand in college and my mom wound up pregnant. When she told him, he wanted nothing to do with me," she says with a shrug and I grip the steering wheel tighter.

"His loss."

"Thanks," she says quietly.

"Do you like it? Translating?" I ask her as I finish off the last of my burger.

"I used to love it. The traveling and being useful, but lately, it's just gotten monotonous. I guess I'm starting to get sick of hotel rooms and boring business meetings."

"Why don't you settle down somewhere? Couldn't you just work for one company?" I ask as the sign for the Fairmont comes up ahead.

"That's pretty rare," she says as she wipes her hands off with a napkin and tosses it into the now empty bag.

"Why not quit and do something else? Something that you love?" I ask as I pull into the drive.

"I'm good at this and I've already built up a client list. I'm already successful doing this," she says and I mull over her words.

I slow down out front of the doors and she gathers up her purse, turning to me with a smile.

"Thanks for the ride," she says, her hand reaching for the door handle and panic starts to settle in my gut.

I don't know what it is about Edie but my gut is telling me not to let her go and I always trust my gut.

"Hey, um, would you like to get dinner with me before you leave town?"

"Another dinner?" She asks me with a cheeky smile as she shakes the empty bag in her hand.

"A real dinner. Somewhere where we sit down and eat food on plates. With silverware."

Her smile softens along with her eyes and she nods.

"I'd like that."

"I'll pick you up tomorrow night at 6 pm," I tell her and she nods, grabbing my phone from the cupholder and typing her name and number into it.

"Call me if you change your mind."

"I won't," I promise her and she gives me one last smile as she hops out of the truck.

I watch her walk into the hotel before I crank the engine and head towards my place. My hands sweat the whole way. Where the heck do people go on dates?

I briefly consider texting Sam or Atlas but either way it will get back to Mischa and I don't want to deal with it. Guess I'll just have to do some research on my own.

4

E die

WHEN I WOKE up at 9 am I already had a text message from Nico. I fall back against my mountain of pillows and smile as I open the text and start to read.

NICO: I forgot to ask last night if you had any food allergies or if you were hungry for anything.

HE SENT it a couple of hours ago and I wonder what kind of crazy person I'm going out with tonight. Who in their right mind wakes up before at least 9 am willingly? My stomach growls at the thought of food and I kick off the covers, tossing my phone on the bed as I head into the shower to get ready for the day.

I rush through my routine and pull on a pair of jeans and a t-shirt before I grab the hotel keycard and my purse and head out the door. I love my days off, where I don't have to dress up and look put together. The casual attire is more me and I wiggle my toes in my flip flops, wondering what I have to wear for my date tonight. Speaking of our date, I text Nico back as I ride down in the elevator.

EDIE: No food allergies but I do have one request.

NICO: Name it.

EDIE: Someplace casual. I'd prefer not to dress up since all I have is my work clothes.

NICO: Done.

EDIE: 6 pm right?

NICO: Yeah is that still okay?

EDIE: Perfect! See you then.

NICO: See you soon, Edie.

I HEAD into a cute little café close to my hotel and order coffee, a breakfast sandwich, and pastry at the counter before I take a seat by the window. I spend my morning, enjoying the sunshine and people watching. I've never been to Pittsburgh before so after breakfast I walk around the city. After a couple of hours, I start to regret wearing flip flops and I stop at a park bench, grabbing a soft pretzel before I sit down.

I'm about two bites into my pretzel when I spot a familiar head of shaggy brown hair. Nico is at a bench a few feet away, his pencil moving over a sketch pad and I smile as he chews on his bottom lip, his brows furrowing as he concentrates.

The pencil looks ridiculous in his big bear paw of a hand but it only endears him to me more. Before I can second guess myself, I stand and head over to his bench. He doesn't look up when I sit down and I use his distracted state to peek over at what he's drawing. It's the sketch of a woman, the curves of her body like water on the page.

"You're really talented," I say and his hand pauses as he looks over, his hazel eyes meeting mine.

"Thanks."

"I forgot what a chatterbox you are," I tease and his lip quirks up on one side.

"What are you doing here?" He asks, tucking his pad away.

"Just exploring the city."

"Have you eaten lunch yet?" He asks as he tucks his pencils away in his backpack.

I wave my soft pretzel at him and he frowns.

"You need to eat more than that," he argues.

"Nah, this will be enough."

He frowns harder at that and before I know what's happening, he's got his backpack over one shoulder and he grabs my hand, dragging me after him. I stumble in my flip flops and he scowls at them slightly. Before I know what's happening, his arms are wrapped around me and he picks me up, cradling me against his chest.

"I can walk! You'll hurt your back carrying me."

"You're not heavy," he says softly and my cheeks flame.

"Yes, I am," I say looking away self-consciously.

"Not to me. You're perfect," he says in his low gravelly voice.

"No, I'm not. Put me down before you hurt yourself."

Nico rolls his eyes at that. "You'll hurt your feet or yourself running around the city in those," he says nodding toward where my feet are dangling over his arm.

I shrug, taking a bite of my pretzel and offering it to him. He takes a bite, his tongue licking up some stray salt on his lips and I almost choke on my own bite. Why is that so hot? He grumbles low in his throat and the vibrations travel through my body, ratcheting my desire up another notch.

"I think you should put me down," I whisper but he just keeps walking.

I'm fluent in five different languages and I'm supposed to be this great communicator but I still can't understand Nico. He walks calmly, his eyes straight ahead.

We reach his truck a few minutes later and I let out a sigh of relief. Well not relief since my body still feels wound tight. It feels like I have another pulse point between my legs and it only beats louder as Nico's hands grip my waist and he helps me into the passenger seat.

"Where are we going?" I ask when he slips into the driver's seat.

"I'll give you the driving tour of Pittsburgh and then I'm going to feed you."

"It's a little early for dinner," I say, looking at the dashboard and seeing that it's only 2:45 pm.

He doesn't answer me, just pulls out of the parking lot and onto the main street. We pass by my hotel and he heads further downtown. I haven't been through this part of town and I smile and look out the window as he points out some of the sights. He doesn't make much small talk if we're stopped but he does answer any of my questions. I love listening to the sound of his voice. It's soothing and before I know it, my head is lolling against the window. The last thing I remember is him pointing out his old neighborhood before my eyes drift shut and I'm out.

5

Nico

EDIE FALLS ASLEEP RIGHT as we're turning around to head back to her hotel and I smile, listening to her soft snores as I fight traffic back downtown. Traffic is getting bad and it's already close to 5 pm so I pull into the parking lot of one of Max's restaurants. I know that he's here since his car is in the lot and he'll be able to get me food fast.

I park and take one last look at Edie. She's still fast asleep in the passenger seat so I sneak out of the truck, closing the door as quietly as I can before I head inside. I stop at the hostess stand and ask if Max is in. She turns to go get him and that's when I see Sam sitting at the bar. I almost turn and walk back out but she's already seen me and Max is already headed my way too.

"Hey, Nico," They say as they stop in front of me.

"Hey, I was wondering if I could put an order for takeout in."

"Sure, you know we can get you whatever you want here, man," Max says with an easy smile.

He calls a waitress over and hands me a menu. It's an Italian place so I order a little of everything, not knowing exactly what Edie wants. The waitress walks away and Sam and Max stand there.

"That's a lot of food. Even for you," Sam says, eyeing me suspiciously.

"It's not just for me," I mumble.

"Oh yeah? Who are you feeding?" Max asks as he wraps his arm around Sam.

"This girl."

"Where is she?" Max asks, looking around like she might materialize out of thin air.

"In my truck."

"Is she there willingly?" Sam asks and I glare at her.

"Yes. She's my date," I say and then I want to take the words back.

Sam and Max both perk up at those words and I bite back a groan.

By some miracle, the waitress comes back with my food then.

"What do I owe you?" I ask, reaching for my wallet.

"On the house," Max says with a smile and I have a feeling that I'll be paying for this later.

"Thanks," I say with a nod before I take the bags and head back to my truck.

Edie is still asleep and I set the food by her feet before I back out of the spot and head toward her hotel. It takes me another twenty minutes to fight traffic up to her hotel. Edie wakes up right as I pull into the hotel parking lot.

"What smells so good?" She asks sleepily and I smile at how adorable she is.

"Italian," I say, nodding to the bags by her feet.

"Yum, I love Italian," she says, sitting up and licking her lips.

"Did you want to go out for dinner? You just seemed tired and I didn't want you to have to change or anything if you'd rather stay in. We can go to my place. I just didn't want to assume..." I trail off as I realize that I'm rambling and turn to find Edie grinning at me.

"I'd love it if you would come up with me." She says and I smile back at her, finding a parking spot.

I carry the bags in one hand as she leads me up to her room. She unlocks the door and lets me in, rushing around to pick up some clothes that are laying around and to make the bed. I set the food on the table in the corner and pull a chair out for Edie. She collapses into it and I take the chair across from her, pulling out utensils and takeout containers.

She pulls one closer, moaning as she lifts the lid and inhales the garlic and tomatoes. She digs in and I have to look away. I pull over my own takeout container and grab a plastic fork, spearing a ravioli and popping it into my mouth.

"You know," she says after a minute, "I was a little surprised that you asked me out."

"Why? You're gorgeous," I state, my brow furrowing as I try to figure out how she could think that I wasn't interested.

"It's just that I think you said, like three words to me the whole time I was at Eye Candy last night."

"I don't really talk that much," I mumble and I can feel my cheeks start to pinken.

"Why is that?"

I pop another bite into my mouth, stalling for time but when I look up, she's watching me expectantly.

"Both of my parents are therapists and I learned early on that they were analyzing every word that I said so I just started talking less. They meant well and I know that they love me. I think that maybe they just couldn't turn it off but it still got annoying. I mean I was always shy but I'd prefer to not be psychoanalyzed."

She mulls over my response for a minute before she nods slightly and starts eating once again.

"Did you have a good childhood?" She asks and I nod.

"Want to elaborate" She asks with a smile and I duck my head.

"Sorry. Force of habit," I mumble.

"It's okay. I like the strong, silent, brooding type," she quips.

"I'm not brooding," I mumble and she laughs.

"Tell me about your childhood," she demands and I stuff another bite in my mouth.

"It was fine. My parents loved me and we were well off. I was happy," I say, wondering what else she wants from me.

She nods, popping the last of her breadstick in her mouth.

"What about you?" I ask.

"Me? Mine was okay. Maybe a little lonely at times. We traveled around quite a bit and I loved exploring all those new places but it got old making new friends every few years, especially when you knew that you would be leaving again soon."

She seems sad when she talks about it and my heart clenches at the hint of loneliness I can hear in her voice.

"I'm sorry," I murmur and she looks up at me with a faint smile.

"It wasn't all bad. I got my love of languages and my career path from it so there's something."

We pile our empty boxes back in the bag and Edie leans back in her chair.

"So, what's for dessert?" She asks with a cheeky grin.

"You," I blurt out before I can stop myself.

"I was hoping you would say that."

I strip off my shirt as I prowl closer to her, letting my eyes roam over her. She stares up at me with hungry eyes and I grin when they dip lower, taking in my wide chest and bulging biceps. She licks her lips as my hands drop to the button on my jeans and I tugs them off, taking my boxer briefs with them. My long, hard cock springs free, pointing right at her and I think her eyes just about bulge out of her head when she gets a good look at my size.

"I'm never going to be able to fit that inside of me," She whispers.

"Yeah, you will," I assure her as I grab her ankle and pull.

Her back bounces off the bed and she lets out a squeak as I grab her jeans and pull them off, tossing them on the floor next to my clothes.

"Lose the shirt, Edie," I order as I spread her legs and settle between them.

Her hands reach for the hem of her t-shirt but she seems to forget what she was going to do when my tongue licks up her center, splitting her folds and dipping inside of her. Her breathing turns to pants almost instantly and she drops her shirt, gripping my hair instead.

"Nico, Nico, Nico," she chants as her hips start to rock against my mouth.

I reach up and grab her hips, pinning them against the bed as my tongue circles her hard clit.

"Fuck!" She shouts up to the ceiling, her legs starting to tremble as her orgasm starts to flow through her.

I keep giving her slow licks as she comes down and she blinks her eyes open slowly, a blissed out smile on her lips as she starts to raise up on her elbows to look down at me. I'm not done with her yet though. She only gets an inch off the bed before my lips wrap around her clit and I suck it into my mouth. Her back hits the mattress with a thud and she sucks in a breath as my tongue moves back and forth over her nub. She's still on edge after her first orgasm and it doesn't take long before she's coming against my mouth all over again.

I still don't stop though and as she comes a second time, I push one thick finger inside of her. Her pussy clenches around the digit and her back arches. I hook my finger, rubbing against that spot deep inside of her that has her seeing stars. I need to get her nice and wet before I try to shove my cock in her and I grin as her legs start to tremble once again. My tongue starts to give her clit long slow licks and she comes again. She's shaking and sweaty when I finally start to climb up her body.

"I thought I told you to take off your shirt," I say as I grab the hem and do it for her.

I settle between her legs, the tip of my cock nudging against her opening and she spreads her legs wider, showing me just how much she wants me. I start to push my big thick cock inside of her and her fingernails dig into my biceps as I stretch her wide around me. She's so wet but that still doesn't make taking me any easier. I look into her eyes as I finally bottom out inside of her and I swear both of our breaths catch. I've never felt so connected to anyone before in my life and it feels like our hearts are beating in sync.

I pull my hips back and she lifts her thighs, wrapping

them around my hips as I start to push back into her. My head dips and I lick her nipples one at a time as my pace starts to pick up. I get lost in her then as my body teeters on the verge of orgasm. Her thighs clamp down around my hips, her heels digging into my ass and I can tell that she's about to come again. She opens her mouth to scream and her pussy clenches around my cock. As she floods my length, I let go, coming with her.

When we finally come back down to Earth, she's still wrapped tight around me. I lean down, kissing her lips softly as I start to rock inside her once more.

6

E die

THE LAST SIX months have flown by and Nico and I are still going strong. This is my longest relationship and if I'm being honest, I had expected it to fizzle out. I mean long distance relationships never work, right? Well, somehow, ours does. We talk and text and FaceTime daily and I stop by Pittsburgh every chance I get. We spend however many days I have there wrapped up in each other and then I leave for the next city.

Leaving has gotten harder and harder to do. It feels like I leave a small part of myself back there with him every time I board a plane and I'm always in a funk for a day or two after I've left. I'm also usually sore for a day or too as well.

It's been two days since I last slept with Nico and I think I'm still walking funny. That guy is big all over and he certainly knows how to use it. You'd think that after six months of seeing each other that I would be used to it but nope. My whole body tingles every time I picture his big body coming down over me. He's so quiet but in the bedroom he's pure alpha. He likes to throw me down on the bed, strip my clothes off and ravish me. I've laid awake the last two nights trying to recreate some of the things he did with his mouth between my legs but my fingers can't compare to that man's tongue.

I feel my body growing flushed and I try to clear thoughts of Nico and his magical body from my head. I'm in a boardroom in Chicago and I should be focused on my client but I keep getting distracted. Every time I shift in my chair, the beard burn that Nico left on the inside of my thighs reminds me of the things we did together that night.

"Haben Sie schon die Zahlen für das letzte Quartal?" My client asks and I force my brain away from Nico and back into this room. I quickly translate the German, asking the other side of the table if they have the numbers from last quarter yet.

I force myself to focus on the meeting and luckily for me, it only lasts another half hour. I stand and push my chair in, folding my hands in front of me and I translate the goodbyes and file out after my clients. They all talk amongst themselves as we ride down in the elevator and I nod goodbye to them as they head toward their car and I head in the other direction. My hotel is only a few blocks away and it's a beautiful day. I wish that I hadn't worn heels after the first block. *Or that Nico was here to carry me.*

When I get back to the hotel, I pick up the room service menu. I'm too tired to change and go out for food and I just want to eat some greasy food, take a shower, and pass out. I place my order and then strip off my clothes, heading into the bathroom. As the steam fills the room, I look at myself in the mirror.

A small smile plays around my lips as I take stock of all of the love bites that Nico left all over my breasts. I run my fingers over the marks, my eyes drifting to half-mast as my fingers toy with my nipples. Steam blurs my image in the mirror and I bite my bottom lip as I let myself remember that night.

Nico was on me as soon as I walked in the door. I yelped as he picked me up and pinned me between him and the wall, his hard length rubbing against me as he attacked my mouth.

"I missed you," he groans against my mouth and I grin.

"I missed you too," I say before I kiss him, dipping my tongue into his mouth and sucking on his tongue until he moans.

His hands pull at our clothes and he sets me down long enough to tug off our jeans and underwear before he's got me pinned once again.

"I need you. I swear I'll be gentler next time," he says as he thrusts up and into me.

We both groan as he fills me so completely and my head drops back as he starts to move inside of me. I'm so wet and I moan as the sounds of him fucking me fill the hallway. He pounds into me over and over again and my nails dig into his shoulders as my orgasm starts to bear down on me.

"That's it, Edie. Come all over me," Nico orders and I let out a sob, my back arching.

I open my mouth to scream and-

"Room service!" Comes a call and I snap out of my daydreams.

My clit pulses and I jerk away from the wall I was leaning at, pulling my fingers out from between my legs as I hurry to shut off the shower and grab the robe hanging on the back of the door.

I answer the door and thank them as they place the food on the table for me. I tip the guy and then shut and lock the door after him. My body is still on edge and I debate if I should finish what I started or eat my food before it gets cold.

That's when my phone rings and I know before looking that it's him. He calls me every night around the same time. He told me the first day that that was when he usually took his break at work and I love that he wants to talk to me in his free time. We've been texting every day too but I know that every night he'll call and we'll get to talk for half an hour.

"Hey," I say as I answer the call and fall back on the bed.

"Edie," he says in that sweet way of his. The one that makes shivers race down my spine.

"Are you on your break?" I ask him and he grunts.

"What did you do today?" He asks and I tell him about the board meeting this afternoon.

"Are you eating?" He asks next and I smile because he always asks this.

"My food just got here before you called. I was going to take a shower but... I got distracted," I say after a second.

"Distracted by what?" He asks, his deep voice coming out deeper as I start to pant.

"I can't stop thinking about you. About the other night," I admit and I hear him let out a small moan.

"I can't stop thinking about you either," he admits and a smile tugs at my lips.

My mind flashes back to the first time we ever had this conversation. I had told him that I had fun the other night and then he had asked for more.

"I promise, I'll call you if I'm ever back in town."

"I want more. I like you. A lot. I was... I was wondering if you

*wanted to do this long distance thang?" He blurts out and I can't
stop grinning.*

*"Yes, I'd like that," I say and I can hear him let out a sigh of
relief. "Wait, did you just say thang?" I ask, replaying his words
in my head.*

*He groans, the sound causing my body to tingle. "I've been
spending way too much time with Mischa and Indie," he
mumbles and I laugh.*

*"Who's Mischa and Indie? Friends?" I ask as I push off the
bed and head over to my food.*

*"More like an annoying little brother and his girl," he says
and I sit down at the table and pick up my fork, tucking into my
alfredo and Caesar salad as he tells me about his family at Eye
Candy Ink.*

I blink back to the present and listen to him tell me how
everyone at the shop is starting to notice how much he's
been on his phone. It's weird to know so much about people
that I've never met but I can't help but laugh when I hear
how Mischa has been teasing him.

"I can't wait to see you again, Edie," he says, his voice
coming out deep with longing and my whole body tightens.
I love that he seems to have forgotten that I just left
yesterday morning. It's nice to know that he misses me as
much as I miss him.

"I can't wait to see you either," I tell him as I finish my
dinner and stare out the window at the nighttime sky.

7

N^{ico}

I CAN HEAR SAM, Mischa, Atlas, and Zeke all talking about me behind the counter but I ignore them, focusing on the text that just came in from Edie.

"He's *smiling*," Sam says in disbelief and I want to roll my eyes.

"And texting. He hates texting. Every time I send him a message he messages back saying unsubscribe," Mischa says and I grin as I hear Zeke laugh.

I know without looking that Zeke is trying to remember that so he can do it to Mischa later. I shift in my chair in the lobby, typing a reply to Edie as they continue to try to figure out what's going on.

"Who could he possibly be talking too? Everyone he knows is here," Atlas asks.

"Maybe he's got a girl," Zeke says.

"A girl?!?" Mischa says, his outburst so loud that my head snaps up on instinct.

My face flame and I know that my cheeks must be a rosy pink right now. Zeke reaches out, grabbing Mischa before he can dive over the front counter and I give Zeke a thankful look and Mischa a pitying one, shaking my phone slightly at him.

"You keeping secrets, Nico?" Sam asks, a gleeful look in her eyes as she edges her way toward the gate. I glare at her because she's the only one who knows about my date the other week.

"You have a girlfriend?" Mischa asks in disbelief.

"Yeah, and I didn't even need any advice from Eye Candy Ink's resident romance expert," I say drily and Mischa laughs.

"When are we going to get to meet her?" Zeke asks, his arms still wrapped tightly around Mischa's shoulders.

"You should have invited her last night," Atlas says, typing away on his phone. I know without looking that he's texting Darcy and telling her about my weird behavior and potential girlfriend.

"She's out of town a lot," I mumble, shoving my phone in my pocket and standing up as Sam sneaks closer to me.

"Ohhhh, I see what's going on here," Mischa says and I turn to see him relax in Zeke's hold. Zeke drops his hold, leaving one arm draped over his shoulders in case he needs to hold him back again.

"What?" Atlas asks, looking up from his phone.

"Nico has a "girlfriend"," Mischa says, using air quotes around the word girlfriend.

I roll my eyes. "She's real," I insist.

"Right, she just lives in Canada or something then? Where did you meet? The chat room at CatfishRUs?"

I can't stop the grin from forming at that and I chuckle softly. My eyes cut to Sam and I wonder if she's going to rat me out or not. She shakes her head slightly and I nod back at her. "No, she came in with a client a couple of weeks ago. The night Trixie came in actually."

"When do we get to meet her?" Zeke asks but before I can answer, the front door opens and our first customer of the day walks in. I let out a thankful breath.

"Morning," Sam says with a fake smile as she heads back around to the counter.

"Alright, everyone back to work," Zeke says as he heads back to his room.

"We're not done talking about this," Mischa says, pointing a finger at me and I roll my eyes back at him.

"What's this "girls" name?" He asks as he follows me down the hall and into my room.

"Why are you using quotations around girls?" I ask as Mischa plops down on the table and Atlas leans against the wall.

"Isn't that your client?" I ask Atlas and he pouts slightly.

"Yeah, but I wanted to hear this," he says.

"Get to work, Atti!" Zeke calls from across the hall and I smile as I take a seat at my desk.

"I'll fill you in later," Mischa says and Atlas grins before he turns and leaves.

"So?" Mischa prods and I look over my shoulder at him.

"What?"

"What's "her" name?" He asks and I chuckle.

"I'm not sure you know how to use quotations," I inform him and he hops off the table, coming around and leaning against my desk.

"I can get Indie to look into this and find out," he says and I sigh. "Well, I can if there is "in fact" a "real" girl," he says with a grin and I can't help but laugh at his random use of air quotes.

"She's real. Her name is Edie. Leave me alone," I say and he grins at me.

"Let me know if you need any tips! I'll send you those articles too," he says as he heads for the door.

"Please don't," I call after him and I smile as I hear him laugh all the way back to his own room.

8

E die

Nico and I are nailing this long-distance relationship thang. Yes, I do still tease him about that, although he has made me promise that I will never say it around Mischa or Indie.

Even though our schedules change daily, we've fallen into a rhythm. We text almost constantly, starting when we wake up in the morning. He calls me on his lunch break and then we try to facetime before bed every night. On the days that I'm traveling or he has a late client, we make up for it the next day.

It's hard for me to remember which city I'm in everyday but Nico always seems to know. I love how he seems to hang on my every word. I've lost count of the nights that I've fallen asleep still talking to him. We both seem desperate to learn everything that we can about the other.

Nights are spent learning more about each other and then sexting. I still can't beat the way Nico did things to my body but I make do and hearing his voice helps to push me over the edge every single time. I think that part of it is that he still doesn't say much but he does when we're sexting. Hearing him detail all of the things that he wants to do to me in that low, raspy, voice does most of the work for me. I swear, I could get off just laying here listening to him talk dirty to me.

He wouldn't let me get away with that though. He loves listening to me describe what I'm doing to myself, telling him how wet I am and how close I am to coming. I always finish with his name on my lips and his groans ringing in my ears.

It's still not the same though and so I decided two weeks ago that the first break I had, I was going back to Pittsburgh. I want to spend the night in his bed, letting him do all of the things that he's said to me over and over again.

Things have changed in the last few days though. We haven't been sexting or talking on the phone so much, mainly because I seem to have gotten sick somehow. It's the strangest thing, I feel nauseous in the morning when I first wake up, but then by noon, I'm back to normal. I'm so tired by the end of the night that I pass out. I even fell asleep before he called one night and woke up with about a hundred missed calls and texts from Nico asking if I was okay. I had called him back right away and told him I was feeling run down and a little sick and he had urged me to take some time off and relax. He sent me chicken noodle soup for dinner that night and I had devoured it as we talked.

I haven't been able to shake this flu thing though and

I've noticed some other symptoms. The other symptoms don't match up with the flu and so that's why I'm here at this drugstore at 6 am, buying a pregnancy test. Well, buying three pregnancy tests.

I pay and take the bag, practically running back to the hotel and into the bathroom. I hurry to open the boxes and read the instructions before I sit down and start taking the tests. Those three minutes seem like the longest of my life and I have a feeling before I even look at the tests what the results will be.

How am I going to tell Nico? What will he say? How will he react to the news? How am I reacting to the news?

Thoughts race through my head and I wonder what the heck I'm going to do as I stand from the edge of the tub and walk over to where the tests are lined up on the counter. I scrunch my eyes shut, taking a deep breath as I open my eyes and look down at the tests.

Positive, positive, positive, they're all positive.

Deep down, I knew they would be and I look up at my reflection in the mirror.

What do I do now? I've always wanted to be a mom and have a family of my own so I'm obviously keeping it but what am I going to do about my job? I can't travel constantly with a baby in tow. What will Nico say? Will he be happy? Will this be too much for us? I really like him; I don't want to lose him.

I pick up my phone, intending to call him and tell him but then I realize that maybe this should be something I tell him in person. I'm flying out to see him tomorrow afternoon. I'll think of how to tell him on the plane.

I pull on my work clothes, sipping some water as I mentally make lists of everything I need to do to get ready for our little one. By the time I'm heading into the conference room for today's meeting, I'm actually feeling excited about all of this.

I just hope that Nico feels the same way.

9

N ico

WORST DAY EVER.

I had to work late tonight and I'm already annoyed that I missed my phone call with Edie. She hasn't been feeling well the last few days and I wanted to check in on her but instead I'm stuck here with this dumb asshole.

He's another VIP client, some television actor from California that flew all the way here to get tattooed by me. I was hoping that when I messaged him and explained that I wasn't traveling to do tattoos right now that he would be put off but instead, he boarded his private jet and flew all the way out here.

Him and his entourage showed up about four hours ago, half of them drunk and I wanted more than anything to turn them away. I know that Zeke would have had my back but I was worried that this guy would bash Eye Candy Ink every-where he could and I didn't want to do anything to hurt the shop so I sucked it up. Right now I'm kind of wishing that I had turned him away.

His tattoo was actually pretty creative and I was excited to draw something up for him. Then the actual tattooing started and I found it harder and harder not to roll my eyes. The dude winced every time my tattoo machine even turned on. My needle didn't even have to be touching him and he was saying he needed a break. I'm a patient man but even I have my limits and when an hour and half, two hour tattoo tops is going on four hours, I've long since lost my patience.

"Dude, seriously?" I growl when he once again jerks away from me before my needle can even touch him.

"It hurts, man," he whines and I bite back a growl.

"It doesn't hurt as much as you're making it look like," I mumble under my breath and the guy shoots a glare over his shoulder at me.

I can't believe that I'm missing my girl for this. The shop is getting ready to close and I see Mischa shoot an annoyed look at some of my client's entourage when he tries to slip by in the hall to check out with Sam. By now, Edie is prob-ably fast asleep. She's been so tired lately and I make a mental note to send her something as a pick me up tomorrow morning.

Mischa comes back to let me know that he walked Sam to her car and I nod. He leans against my wall, eyeing some of the guys in the room and I have a feeling that he'll be sticking around until I'm finished. Atlas joins him a minute later and they both stand guard in my doorway.

I ignore them, getting back to work. I have to basically pin the guy down to finish the tattoo but after another hour, he's bandaged up and ready to leave. He passes me some cash and I know without looking that it was not worth the last couple of hours. *Fucking VIP clients.* I walk them to the door and lock it behind them.

I'm headed back to my room to clean up but I freeze in the doorway when I see Atlas and Mischa already have it covered. Mischa tosses some disinfectant wipes in the trash as Atlas finishes putting away my machine and I smile gratefully at both of them.

"Figured you'd want to get "back" to "your" girlfriend," Mischa says with a wry grin and I laugh.

"She's real, Mischy. No need for the air quotes."

"Who the hell told you about Mischy?" He asks, shooting Atlas a dirty look.

Atlas holds up his hands, opening his eyes wide and trying his best to look innocent.

"I know it was you, Atti," Mischa mumbles but he shakes it off and turns back to face me.

"How are things going with your girl? With Zeke and Trixie getting matching tattoos, you're the last of us left."

"Yeah, I heard Indie was talking you into matching tattoos too. I thought those were the "kiss of death"," I tease him.

"In case you were wondering, that was the correct way to use air quotes," Atlas says as he pulls his phone out of his jeans pocket. I'm sure he's texting Darcy and letting her know he'll be home soon.

"Indie and I are solid. Couple goals," he says making the hashtag sign with his hands and Atlas and I both laugh at that.

"If both of your girls are at home, then what the hell are you still doing here?" I ask as I grab my backpack from next to my desk and start to walk with them up front.

"Wanted to make sure you're alright. You've been glued

to your phone for weeks and we feel like we've barely seen you. You missed the boy's night the other day and we just wanted to check in with you," Atlas says and Mischa nods.

"I'm fine," I promise them. "I'll make the next boy's night."

"Great! It's next Tuesday," Mischa says, clapping me on the shoulder.

"I have-" I open my mouth but Mischa cuts me off.

"You promised," he yells over his shoulder as he takes off running toward his car. He's got his hand wrapped around Atlas's elbow and he drags him after him. Atlas waves bye at me and I chuckle as I return it. Guess I'll be cancelling dinner with my parents next week.

I turn to head to my truck when a cab pulls up in front of the shop and I stop, waiting to see who would be arriving so late. My lungs seem to freeze when the backdoor opens and Edie steps out, a small bag in her hand.

I take the two steps separating us and pull her into my arms as my lips land on hers. I didn't realize just how much I missed seeing her until I saw her again. We break apart when the cab driver clears his throat and I reach for my wallet, passing him some money and slamming the door closed.

I take her bag from her and thread my fingers through hers as I lead her over to my truck.

"What are you doing here?" I ask as I open the passenger door and toss both of our bags in the back.

"I wanted to see you. I need to tell you something," she says and she seems nervous.

She wrings her fingers together and I frown, taking both of her hands in mine and stepping closer to her as she leans against the passenger seat.

"You can tell me anything."

"I'm pregnant," she blurts and my fingers squeeze around hers as shock fills me at her words.

She blinks up at me and I can see tears forming in her eyes.

"Really?" I ask, a small smile tugging at my lips.

I don't know what is happening. Normally I'm so in control of my emotions but I just went from shock, to happiness, to anxious in about the blink of an eye.

"Yeah. I took like a hundred tests," she says, scanning my face.

"That's the best news," I say as I wrap my arms around her waist and pull her to me.

"You're not... upset?"

"No. Why would I be upset? I'm going to be a father," I say and I barely recognize my voice.

"But we haven't known each other that long and we've only been in the same city for like a third of the time that we've been dating," she says and I pull back to stare into her eyes.

"I don't need time to know how I feel about you. I love you, Edie. I want you to be safe and happy and have everything you ever wanted. Will we have to figure out some stuff? Absolutely. Will we argue about some of that stuff? Probably. But at the end of it all, I don't care about the fights or arguments. I don't care as long as we're together. I wanted a family with you and it might be happening sooner than I expected but that doesn't change that I still want it."

"I love you too," she says before she bursts out into sobs and leans against my chest.

I wrap my arms around her, smoothing my hands down her hair and back and trying my best to comfort her. We probably look crazy to anyone driving by with her crying into my chest and my grinning as I try to calm her down but how could I be anything but happy? I've got my girl here with me after weeks apart and I just found out that I'm going to be a father.

Best day ever.

10

E die

I BLINK my bleary eyes open, squinting against the sunlight streaming into the cozy room. It's bright and I know it must be close to noon. I sit up in the bed, tossing the pale blue comforter away as I swing my legs over the edge. Before I can hop down though, the bedroom door opens and Nico tiptoes in.

I can't stop the smile that forms when I see my big, giant of a man tiptoeing into the room so he doesn't wake me up. He gives me a slight smile and carries over the grocery bags to my side of the bed.

"I ran out and got you some stuff," he says as he starts to pull out suckers and prenatal vitamins, books, and some crackers.

I pick up the suckers and smile when I see their the

Preggo Pops. Nico takes the bag from me and rips it open, unwrapping one for me and passing it back.

"Thanks," I say as I pop it in my mouth.

I look up to see him studying my face and I give him a questioning look.

"Are they working?" He asks, nodding toward the sucker and I grin.

"I think it might take longer than three seconds for me to determine that."

"Right. Well if they do, I can go back and get more. Are you hungry?" He asks as he picks up the prenatal vitamins. "It doesn't say that you have to eat with these, just that it might help," he says and I know that he's about to go get me something to eat before he even turns to leave.

"Maybe just some toast?" I call out after him as I slide off the bed.

He's got a king size bed but it's about four feet off the ground which makes sense since he's so tall but it makes it difficult for me to get in and out and that's before my belly pops out. Nico must have put me to bed last night. Come to think of it, I barely even remember getting to his house.

It was pretty late when we finally got back to his place. These days, 9 pm is past my bedtime and it was closer to 10 pm by the time we got here. I poke around his bedroom for a minute until I find his bathroom. This baby is always pressing on my bladder and I swear I must pee a hundred times a day. I take care of business and then walk out of the bedroom in search of Nico.

His place is nice. All of the walls are painted a soft blue that only serves to make the hardwood floors look darker. I walk down the hallway and notice that everything smells like lemons. I wonder if Nico is making something with them.

I walk out into a sunken living room and look over the couch to see Nico in the kitchen there. He's buttering some toast and I smile when I notice that my stomach isn't revolting like normal.

"Why's this place smell like lemons?" I ask as I walk around and take a seat at the counter.

"Diffuser," he says, nodding toward a little machine sitting on the end table in the living room.

"Huh. You don't seem like the type," I tell him and he gives me a small smile.

"I got it this morning. I was reading and they said that some smells helped with nausea so I got some of the oils and a diffuser. We can move it into the bedroom if it works or get another one."

"You sure seem to know a lot about this pregnancy stuff."

"I stayed up late last night and read a bunch of stuff."

"Of course you did," I say as he slides my plate of toast in front of me.

"Did you want anything else?" He asks as he cleans up some crumbs from the counter.

"If I'm going to be sleeping here when I'm in town, you need to get a shorter bed," I tell him as I take a small bite of the toast. The Preggo Pops seem to be working but I still don't want to push it.

"We'll get a shorter bed. What did you mean, when you're in town?" He asks, coming around and taking a seat next to me at the counter.

"Well I'll still be working until the baby comes," I say trailing off when I see his brow furrow.

"You don't have to work. I want to be there for you while you go through this. I want to be there for all of the doctor appointments and the first kick. We can decorate the nursery together."

He looks so hopeful and I don't want to wipe that expression off his face but I need to work.

"I can be here for all of that. I can make this my home base but I still need to work. I don't have enough in savings to live off of for nine months plus."

"I have money. I want to take care of you, of both of you."

"Remember those arguments you said we were going to have?"

"This isn't an argument. It's a conversation," he insists.

"Okay let's figure out a compromise. Isn't that what couples are supposed to do?"

"According to my parents, we should never compromise because it can lead to anger and regret in relationships. We're supposed to work together to find solutions."

"Okay... then how's this for a solution. I will keep working," I hold my hand up to stop him and he frowns but keeps his mouth shut. "I will only take jobs where I have to be away for three days or less and I will only take one job a week. I'll be here for every doctor appointment and will help with the nursery. After my second trimester, I'll stop working until after the baby comes and then we can reevaluate after that."

He frowns but seems to be considering his words. "Maybe you can find a job here?"

"I've tried but there aren't any. I might be able to get one with a company in New York or maybe Los Angeles but are you going to move?"

"I will if it means we're together," he says right away and my jaw drops. I don't know what I expected but an immediate agreement to move his entire life wasn't quite it.

"You'd really move? Just like that?" I whisper, turning to face him.

"Of course. I love you, Edie. I'd do anything for you, for our family."

Just like last night, I burst into tears and Nico pulls me into his arms. My emotions are out of control lately but Nico doesn't seem to mind. I let him hold me until I calmed down and then I let him carry me back to bed, lay me out on the mattress, and make love to me until I fall asleep again.

11

Nico

I'VE SPENT the past two weeks getting used to having Edie living with me. I thought it would be weird to have someone in my space all of the time but I love it. Edie is funny and smart and even though I've spent six months getting to know her, it feels differently with her actually here.

She was gone for the last three days; in New York this time and I missed her more than I thought. I thought that we were pros at this long-distance thing but it's worse now that I know what it's like to have her here with me all of the time. Her belly is just starting to pop out and she claims to hate it but I've noticed that she can't seem to stop rubbing her hands over it. I can't stop either for that matter.

She missed Sam and Max's wedding and I know that they were both disappointed that she couldn't make it but I promised them that I would introduce her to everyone soon.

Especially now that everyone knows that she's pregnant. Zeke and Trixie told everyone and then I told them that I was going to be a father too.

Everyone is excited for us but now that Edie is back and I've told one of my families, I figure that it's time to tell my other family too. That's where Edie and I are headed now. My parents seemed surprised when they told them that I was seeing someone and that I had news to tell them and they invited us over for dinner right away.

I pull up outside of my childhood home and get out to help Edie out. She looks around and I wonder what she sees when she looks at the two-story cottage. It's been kept up and I smile when I see the rose bushes that my mom planted this season lining the front walk.

"Ready for this?" I ask her as we walk up to the front door.

"As I'll ever be," she says as I open the door and lead her in.

"Mom! Dad!" I call out as we walk inside.

I lead Edie into the kitchen and squeeze her hand before I walk over to give my mom a hug and shake my dad's hand.

"Mom, Dad, this is Edie. Edie, this is my mom and dad," I say, introducing them.

I smile as my mom and dad both step forward and hug Edie, telling her how beautiful she is and how I haven't been able to stop talking about her. Edie laughs at that, giving me a knowing look and I grin down at her.

We sit down for dinner a few minutes later and I groan as the usual interrogation starts up. I watch Edie as they question her, making sure that she's comfortable. As we're clearing away the dishes, Edie pulls me aside and whispers in my ear.

"I can see what you mean. They're nice but I can almost

see them picking apart every word I say. It's like being under a microscope."

"So how long have you two been seeing each other?" My mom asks with a friendly smile.

"About six months," Edie says with a smile and I take a deep breath.

"We actually have something to tell you," I say and Edie slips her hand into mine underneath the table.

"I'm pregnant," Edie says, grinning from ear to ear.

My parents seem shocked but they recover quickly, congratulating us and we spend the rest of dinner talking about babies and everything we need to buy. My parents both seem excited to be grandparents and I'm glad they took it well.

I wrap my arm around her waist and tell my parents I'm going to show her my old room before we have to leave.

I lead Edie upstairs and down the hall into my childhood room. It's still the same as I left it with posters of famous paintings on the walls and some old band posters. My twin size bed is in the corner with a dresser and my closet on the opposite wall. It's not much to see but I wanted to give Edie a bit of a break before we head over to Zeke's place. I promised that I would bring her over to meet everyone and she said she wanted to do it all in one night since we never know what her schedule will be.

"Ready to go?" I ask her, cradling her against my chest.

"Yeah," she says with a yawn and I know that she's starting to get tired.

"Do you want to wait and do it on a different night?" I ask her but she shakes her head.

"I want to meet your family. All of your family," she says with another yawn and I kiss her forehead before I lead her back downstairs.

We say goodbye to my parents before I bundle Edie back in my truck and head back across town to Zeke's warehouse. Edie dozes in the passenger seat on the way there and I hate to wake her but as I pull into Zeke's garage I can already see Mischa and Indie with their faces practically smashed against the windows lining Zeke's apartment.

I roll my eyes at them as I go around to the passenger side and help Edie out of the truck. We've already talked about getting something newer and safer once the birth date gets closer and I know that I need to get Edie her own car so that she isn't always relying on me.

"Are you sure you're ready for this?" I ask her as I help her up the stairs.

She giggles and grins when she sees Mischa and Indie practically bouncing with excitement as we approach.

"Is that Mischa and Indie?" She whispers and I let out a sigh.

"Who else could it be," I groan as Indie jerks the door open and races down the two steps, grabbing Edie and pulling her into a hug.

"We're so glad to meet you!" Indie says as she drags Edie into the apartment and over to the other girls.

Everyone is sitting in the living room and I close the door after me and then head over to join them. Sam is passing Edie and Trixie bags and I lean against the couch armrest as they open up the gift bags.

"We pitched in and got you both some Motherhood Maternity gift cards and some other pregnancy goodies," Darcy says with a sweet smile and Atlas tugs her closer into his side, kissing her forehead.

"Thank you guys," Edie says right as Trixie bursts into tears.

All of the men look taken aback but Edie knows what to do. She wraps her arms around Trixie and hugs her.

"I know, I've been crying almost nonstop too," she tells her and Trixie sniffles into her shirt.

"I can't seem to help it," Trixie says and Zeke comes up next to me, bumping his shoulder with mine as the girls bond over hormones and other pregnancy side effects.

I take a seat at the counter with the guys and we all watch as the girls bring up websites for baby stuff and bond in the living room. When Edie can't stop yawning I know that it's time to go and I slap Mischa and Zeke on the back, waving at Atlas and Max as I get my girl and take her out to the truck.

"I don't want you to leave," Edie murmurs as I buckle her in.

"I'm not going anywhere," I promise her.

"I don't want you to leave your family. We can stay here. I'll move to Pittsburgh permanently."

I lean in and kiss her lips and she smiles sleepily up at me.

"I love you, Edie."

"I love you too, Nico," she whispers against my lips.

I close the door and slip behind the wheel, smiling as I drive my girl home.

12

E die

NICO HAS SEEMED weird the last few days. It's almost like he's nervous about something and I keep trying to relax. My mom comes in tomorrow to meet him and I figure he's just worried about making a good impression with her. I've been telling him that he has nothing to worry about but it hasn't seemed to really help.

Me, on the other hand, well I can't wait for my mom to get here. I still talk to her once a week but I haven't seen her in a few months. We have a standing deal that whenever I take a job in Washington, DC or anywhere close, that we make the time to see each other.

She hasn't seen me since I told her that I was pregnant and I know that she's going to be surprised by my little baby bump already. We're getting close to the second trimester and I know the deal was that I would work until the third trimester but I've been dreading work more and more.

I feel guilty even thinking that. My mom is my hero. She was a single mom who proved all of the critics wrong by raising me and being successful in her career. I always wanted to be like her and I don't know when that dream changed. Maybe it's just the pregnancy hormones that has me wanting to be a stay at home mom instead of trying to conquer the world. I just don't know how to do that without letting her down or feeling like I'm letting myself down.

I've been out of town for the last two days and I know that Nico is still at work. He found me a car, some super safe model with all the bells and whistles and surprised me with it last week. He said I would need it once the baby got here and this way I wouldn't have to take cabs and Ubers everywhere. It had taken a couple of days to get used to driving myself around again but I'm starting to remember how much I love it.

I yawn as I pull onto our street and smile when I see the porch light is on. He always leaves it on for me since most work trips have me getting in late. I pull into the driveway and hit the button for the garage, pulling inside and parking. I had tried to tell him that I could park in the driveway but he insisted. He's such a sweet man.

I yawn again as I pull my bag out of the back and hit the button to close the door. I'm halfway through the door when the scent of flowers hits me. It's almost overpowering and I wrinkle my nose to stop from sneezing.

"Shit, I forgot how sensitive your smelling is. Hold on, baby," Nico says as he hurries around the room. Picking up bouquets and shoving them into the pantry.

I watch him for a minute before I look around the place. It looks like every available surface is decked out in flowers and candles. There's food on the counter and an enormous amount of balloons in the corner for some reason.

"Better?" Nico asks as he walks over to me and takes my bag from me.

"What is all of this?" I ask as he leads me over to the center of the living room.

He sets my bag down, wiping his palms on his jeans as he shifts nervously. I watch as he takes a deep breath and then sinks down on one knee in front of me.

"Edie Marie West, I love you. You're the best thing that ever happened to me. Will you marry me?" He asks as he pulls out a small box.

He opens the box but I'm not paying attention. I can't seem to tear my eyes away from his face. The now familiar tears start and Nico's eyes fill with worry as he watches me.

"Yes," I whisper, wiping away the tears.

Nico stands and pulls me against his chest.

"You don't have to, you know."

I laugh, more tears falling as I look up at him.

"I want to," I promise him and he smiles softly down at me.

"I love you, Edie. More than anything," he says as he slides the ring onto my finger.

"I love you t-" I start to say when the pantry door bursts open and Mischa and Indie poke their heads out.

"What did she say?" He asks and I laugh when I see they're each holding armfuls of flowers. Nico must have just shoved them at him when he put them in there.

"You're supposed to wait until Nico says to come out," Atlas whispers, poking his head out of the front closet. Darcy pulls him back in, rolling her eyes at their antics.

"Are we supposed to come out? I can't hear anything

back here," Zeke says from the spare bedroom and I hear Trixie giggle.

"That's because you're so old, Dad," Mischa yells and the guest room door opens.

Zeke holds Trixie's hand as they walk down the hallway and he stops to knock on the bathroom door. Sam and Max's heads poke out and I can't help but laugh.

"What did she say?" Sam asks, elbowing past Zeke and racing over to my side.

"I said yes!" I say as I hold up my hand.

All of the girls are on me then and we laugh and hug each other. I watch the boys all go over to congratulate Nico before they switch and I yelp when Mischa almost tackles me.

"I'm glad he found you," he whispers in my ear and I hug him harder.

"I'm glad I found him."

Atlas, Max, and Zeke are all gentler with me and they each whisper welcome to the family to me before we pull apart.

"Let's eat!" Indie says, heading over to the kitchen.

"That's what all of the food is for. I thought maybe you thought that I started eating enough for twenty while I was away.

"No, I told them I was going to propose and they all insisted on helping out. The flowers are from Atlas and Darcy, the food from Sam and Max, those ridiculous balloons, well I think you can guess," Nico says, swatting away some of the balloon strings as we pass underneath the bunch. Mischa and Indie both point at themselves and I grin.

"Yeah, I figured that," I assure them and Indie grins as she passes me a plate.

"Trixie and I got you something but it's at work and a surprise," Zeke says and I smile at both of them.

"Can't wait."

"I know what it is," Mischa says and I have a feeling getting it out of him will be easy.

Zeke shoots him a warning look as he moves around the counter making a plate for Trixie. We all fill our plates and then take seats in the living room to eat and catch up. Everyone looks to me and I realize they're waiting for me to sit before they start to dig in.

"You don't have to wait for me. I need to run to the bathroom anyway. Go ahead and do this thang!" I say with a laugh only to be met with dead silence.

Nico groans and I turn to see Mischa watching him with glee.

"Oh man," Atlas says with a grin and Sam can't say anything because she's already laughing too hard.

I look to Nico with wide eyes, mouthing "sorry" as I head down the hallway and into the bathroom. When I come out a few minutes later they're still giving him crap about it.

"I think it's just that we're the most hip couple in the shop. We're trendsetters!" Mischa says and Indie nods next to him.

"Yeah, that's not it," Nico says in a dry tone and I snort as I sit down next to him.

He passes me my plate and I swear I almost drool as I pick up my fork and dig in. Trixie is on my other side and I turn and ask her how she's doing. Her and I are both about fifteen weeks along and we talk about our symptoms and how excited we are to find out the gender in a few weeks. I have a feeling we'll be having another party just like this once we know what we're having.

After the food is gone, I can barely keep my eyes open

and Nico notices. Of course he does. He still seems to notice everything about me. I thank everyone for coming and for everything and hug them goodbye before Nico takes me to bed. He tucks me in, cradling me against his chest and I feel him kiss my head.

"Love you," I mumble and then I'm out.

13

N ico

EDIE'S MOM comes in today and she's been practically bursting with excitement since we woke up this morning. I still have to work this afternoon but Edie told me that was fine since she wanted some time for just her mom and her anyway.

We're headed to the airport now and I smile as Edie rubs her hand over her little baby bump. She touches it a lot and I can tell that she's excited to become a mom. Hell, I can't wait to be a dad either. I reach over, rubbing my hand along the swell and she smiles at me. I pull off the highway and into the airport terminal and Edie sits up straighter in her seat, her eyes scanning all of the passengers as she looks for her mom.

"There!" She says and I fight traffic over to the curb.

Edie is out of the passenger side and over to a sophisticated woman in her late forties before I can shift into park. I shake my head as I climb out and pop the trunk. I'm still getting used to my new SUV but I know that it was necessary for when the baby gets here.

"Mom, this is Nico. Nico, this is my mom, Susan West," Edie says with a giant smile and I smile as I hold my hand out to her mom.

"Nice to meet you, M'am."

"It's nice to finally meet you too. In person," she says with a sly smile as she nods towards Edie's engagement ring.

"In person?" Edie asks, looking between us as I put her mom's luggage in the back of the car.

"He called me last week to ask for my blessing. I told him that you didn't need my blessing but he said he wanted to be respectful and that he knew it would mean a lot to you if he had it," her mom explains and I turn to see Edie's eyes well up with tears.

I pull her into my arms instantly, rubbing soothing circles on her back as she sniffles into my shirt.

"Remember when I never used to cry?" She asks as she looks up at me.

"Sorta."

She huffs but smiles up at me. "Love you, Nico."

"Love you more," I say as I help her into the car and then grab the door for her mom.

I let the girls catch up as I drive them home and I help carry in the bags before it's time for me to kiss Edie goodbye and head into work. They assure me they'll be fine and that they're just going to hang out here today so I make plans to call in an order for some takeout so that they don't have to cook. Edie's been obsessed with this Italian place and their chocolate cake so I place an order for later today for them.

Work is pretty dead when I get there and Sam waves as I

walk in. She's on the phone so I just wave back and head into my room. I'm going through my papers for today's clients when Mischa wanders into my room. I try my best to hold back my groan but judging from the shit eating grin on his face, he still heard it.

"So..." he starts.

"It was one little slip of the tongue. I regretted it immediately."

He chuckles at that before he hops up on my table.

"Want me to never bring it up ever again?" He asks.

"God yes."

"Indie and I are getting matching tattoos. Do the work and I swear I'll never say anything again."

"Deal. What are you getting?" I ask.

"Don't know yet. Indie is still trying to figure out what she wants and then I'll draw it up for us."

"Alright."

"You going to get one with Edie?" He asks.

"No, I'll get her and the baby's name tattooed on me but I don't think she wants a tattoo."

Mischa gasps in mock outrage and I grin, shrugging in a what can you do kind of way.

"I'll let you know when Indie figures it out," he says as he hops off the table. "Oh, and congrats again, Nico. I'm happy for you, bro."

"What's it going to take for you to never call me bro again?" I ask and he just laughs as he skips back to his room.

I grin as I watch him disappear and then shake my head. I'd never admit it to him but I think of him and Atlas as brothers too.

I'm finishing up with my first client of the day when Zeke comes into my room.

"What's up, boss?" I ask as I grab some bandages and ointment from my desk.

"Got a minute?"

"Yeah, give me just a sec," I say and he nods, wandering back out into the hallway.

I finish up and walk my client up front to pay before I head back to Zeke's office. He's inside and I stop short when I see what else is in there.

"So since we're both going to be dads soon, I thought it might be a good idea to have daycare stuff here. In case you ever need to bring your kid in."

I stare in shock at the two cribs set up along the wall. There's mats and bouncers and a swing and diapers already stacked up along the back wall next to some tattoo supplies.

"Trixie is going to be here with me a lot and so our kid will be here too. I just thought it made sense to have stuff in case you wanted to bring your kid in too. One of us will always be back here with them so it's like built-in babysitting."

I nod and I'm almost embarrassed as my eyes start to get misty.

"Thanks, man," I say, clearing my throat and he just gives me a small smile before he pulls me into a hug, thumping my back.

"There's one more thing," he says as he heads over to his desk and grabs some papers.

He passes them to me and I scan them, my brow furrowing. "What's this?"

"I'm making you a partner of Eye Candy Ink. I probably should have done it a long time ago."

"What? No, you don't need to do that," I insist, trying to hand the papers back to him.

"I'm making everyone a partner. You guys are family, the

best family Trixie and I will ever have and I want you to all be a part of this."

"Yes," Mischa says behind me and I move out of the doorway.

"You think I'm falling for that again?" He asks, crossing his arms over his chest.

"Falling for what?" Atlas asks, coming up behind him and trying to push him forward.

"If I walk into a room with more than one of you in it, it turns into a group hug. So no, I'm not falling for this," he says as he braces his arms on the side of the doorframe.

He looks a bit like a cat trying to avoid going in the bathtub and Atlas grins, nodding at Zeke and me over his shoulder. Zeke and I both lunge for him and Mischa turns, running into Atlas. He ducks down, taking off toward the lobby and I laugh as I watch him run.

"Sam wanted to see you," Atlas tells me, clapping me on the shoulder as I pass him.

"Thanks," I say, turning back to Zeke. "You guys are the best family that I ever had too."

"Awwww!" Mischa says from his hiding place up front and I grin as I head toward him.

"You wanted to see me?" I ask as I walk up behind Sam.

"Yeah, sorry that was your client on the phone earlier. Some family emergency so they had to cancel so you're done for the day. Unless you wanted to wait for walk-ins."

I look around the lobby and see it's still empty.

"I'll take off," I tell her and she nods.

"See you later!" I call as I grab my keys and shut my room door.

"See ya!" They all call back and I grin as I head out to my car.

I change the takeout order to pick up and swing by the

Italian place before I head home. The sun is starting to set and I can see Edie and her mom in the living room curled up on the couches. There's a package by the front door and I smile, knowing that it's the pregnancy pillow that I got for Edie. She was complaining about her back hurting and these are supposed to help.

I head in through the garage door, setting the food on the counter quietly so that I don't disturb them before I turn to grab the package.

Edie sniffles and I freeze in my tracks, my hand on the doorknob.

"I just don't want to let you down. I don't want to be a failure," she cries softly and I'm turning to tell her that she could never be a failure when her mom speaks up.

"I know that you look up to me and that's great, honey, but that doesn't mean that you need to live my life. I needed to work to support us and I wanted to give you a better life. That's why I worked so hard. Settling down doesn't mean settling, Edie. If getting married and staying home with your kids is what you want, then do that. You're not a failure, Edie. You could never be a failure as long as you follow your dreams. So forget about what you think being successful means and answer this question instead. What do you want?"

"Nico," she says instantly and my heart swells in my chest. "He's the best, mom. So sweet and protective and I know that he'll be the best dad and husband. He's so supportive and I know that he'll always encourage me to go after what I want. I don't know what I want to do career wise after I have our baby though."

"Maybe it doesn't matter right now. You've got a great man, you're about to be a mom. You don't have to have it all figured out. Babies change everything so it's okay to take it one day at a time. And like you said, Nico isn't going anywhere and I know that he'll always be there to help you. That man wants nothing more than for you to be happy and it's so obvious. You're going to be just fine, Edie. Just listen to your heart and you'll be great."

"Thanks, mom," she says and as they hug on the couch I head outside and grab the box from the front porch.

I make sure to make lots of noise this time when I come in and I smile when they both turn to face me.

"Hey, I got off early so I picked up some food."

"Chocolate cake?" Edie asks when she sees the bags on the counter.

"Of course," I say as I carry the box over and lean it against the wall in the hallway.

"What's that?" Edie asks as she heads into the kitchen and starts to take out the food.

"A pregnancy pillow. It's supposed to help with your back and cradle your belly when it gets big," I tell her as I head over to help her set out the food.

"You mean when it gets bigger," she says as she grabs the plates.

"No, when it gets big."

"I love you," she says, rising on her tiptoes to kiss me.

I bend down and cradle her face in my hands.

"I love you more."

Her mom watches us with a smile on her face and she nods at me when she catches me watching her. Thank you, she whispers when she comes into the kitchen and I smile wider.

"Trust me. It's my pleasure."

14

E die

SIX MONTHS LATER...

I WADDLE into Eye Candy Ink, smiling at Sam as she waves at me behind the counter. She's on the phone so I head over to one of the chairs to wait until she's done. My ankles are so swollen and I wince as another sharp pain hits my lower back. It's been happening all morning but our doctor told me at our last appointment to expect some Braxton Hicks contractions.

I'm about to lower into a chair when Mischa strolls up to the front, grinning wide when he sees me in the lobby.

"Hey, Mrs. Mitchell!" He says as he heads over to hug me.

Nico and I got married a couple of months ago in a small

ceremony with everyone at Eye Candy Ink, my mom, and Nico's parents. Max had catered and Darcy had insisted on doing flowers so all I had to do was find a dress big enough to fit me and walk down the aisle. Nico had taken me on a honeymoon/babymoon for a week after that and we frolicked in the warm waters in the Bahamas before we came back here and set up the nursery.

I haven't been working for a few months and it's been awesome just focusing on our little one's arrival and on spending more time with Nico and our family. The nursery is all set and we have everything for our son's birth. Well, everything except a name and a car seat. I ordered the car seat but it hasn't come in yet and Nico and I can't decide on a name. He says to just wait until he's born and then see what we feel like and I trust him so that's what we're going to do.

"Hey, Misha," I say opening my arms for a hug.

As soon as his arms wrap around me, another stabbing pain hits and I yelp, bending forward slightly and gripping Mischa's forearms. Shit, that hurt.

"What did you do?" Sam asks, hanging up the phone and standing. Her face is pale and worried but not as much as Mischa's. Mischa looks like he might faint.

"I just hugged her. It wasn't even hard!"

"Ah!" I yelp as another wave of pain crashes over me and I bend forward again, one hand falling to cradle my stomach.

"Uh, Zeke. ZEKE!" Mischa yells when I stay hunched over and I hear heavy footfalls a second later.

"What did you do?" Atlas asks as he almost runs into the gate.

Zeke is right behind him and I can see the alarm on his face when he gets a look at us.

"Okay, can you walk?" He asks me as he comes to my other side. I've still got a death grip on Mischa's forearm with my other hand and I nod slightly.

"Okay, Sam call Nico and tell him to meet us at the hospital. Atlas, go finish that client and Sam will cancel our other ones for the day. Mischa go get your car. It's lower so we'll be able to get in and out of it easier," Zeke barks out orders and everyone springs into action.

"Where's Nico?" I ask as I lean on Zeke and let him half lead, half carry me out to Mischa's car.

"Your car seat came in and he ran up to grab it in between clients," Zeke says, opening the back door and helping me in.

He runs around to the other side and climbs into the back with me, telling Mischa to step on it.

Mischa peels out and I wince, groaning as another contraction hits.

"Knock knock?" Mischa says and Zeke and I both turn to look at him like he's crazy.

"What?" I ask.

"Knock, Knock," he says again.

"Mischa, what the hell are you doing?" Zeke asks, grabbing my hand and letting me squeeze as another contraction hits.

"I don't know, panicking?" Mischa says, his voice coming out rushed and high like he's nervous.

I laugh at that and Zeke rolls his eyes.

"Just pay attention to the road, kid."

"You got it, dad."

"Do you remember your breathing?" Zeke asks me and I nod.

"Okay, in, in, out, in, in, out," he says, mimicking what they taught us in birth class.

I do it for a second, gripping Zeke's hand tighter as pain floods me again.

"Mischa, what the heck are you doing? The breathing isn't for you! Knock it off, you sound like you're going to hyperventilate!" Zeke barks and I finally notice that Mischa was doing the breathing with me.

Mischa squeals into the parking lot, pulling right up to the front door and he throws his driver's side door open before he's even got the car in park.

"Come on, I'll help you out," Zeke says, coming around to my side while Mischa sprints inside to grab someone.

"Thanks," I say at the same time I hear tires squeal to a stop behind us.

Nico rushes over to my side and takes over for Zeke. He's got the hospital bag in one hand and he lifts me up, carrying me inside with ease.

"I'll get your car," Zeke calls over to him and Nico nods in thanks as he puts me into the wheelchair that a nurse brought out.

"I'm sorry I wasn't there. I got the car seats and then went home to surprise you with dinner. I was just walking in the door when Sam called and told me," Nico says, smoothing back my hair.

"I went to the shop to surprise you," I tell him with a small laugh.

It gets cut off as another contraction hits and Nico immediately takes over, grabbing my hand and breathing with me. He helps me get settled in the bed and into my hospital gown, rubbing my back and letting me squeeze the hell out of his hand and yell as the pain ratchets up.

"I called your mom and my parents. Your mom is getting a flight as we speak and my parents are headed over now," he tells me as he braids my hair back away from my face. He knows it drives me crazy when it hangs in my eyes and I smile up at him.

"I love you," I tell him and he tips my chin up, kissing me quickly.

"I love you more."

Our doctor walks in after that but I see Mischa, Indie, Zeke, and Trixie standing outside the door. Trixie flashes me a thumbs up as she rubs her own baby bump and I try my best to grin back at her.

"Ready to have a baby?" The doctor asks as she wheels closer to me.

"Yeah! Let's do this thang!" Mischa yells outside the door.

"Security!" Nico yells back and I laugh.

"Yeah, let's have a baby," I say, squeezing Nico's hand as the doctor tells me to start pushing.

The next two hours are hell but I know that at the end of it, our baby boy will be here and our family will all be out in the waiting area waiting to meet him. I don't know how I got so lucky but maybe I need to send Pascal Gagne a thank you card for introducing me to my big teddy bear of a husband and his wild, crazy, completely loveable family.

ico

Eɪɢʜᴛᴇᴇɴ Yᴇᴀʀs Lᴀᴛᴇʀ...

Iᴛ's prom night and everyone is crowded into Zeke and Trixie's place as we take pictures and get ready to send our kids off. My son, Zeke, is taking Zeke and Trixie's eldest daughter, Nicole. They've been dating for about a year now and while Zeke wasn't exactly thrilled that his daughter was dating, he did admit that he was glad she was seeing someone that he trusted instead of some punk.

As you can imagine, Mischa had a field day when they told us they were seeing each other. He's laid off the teasing in the last few days and as I watch his son make goo goo eyes at Sam's daughter, I have a feeling I know why. He watches his son with a scowl, swearing under his breath when his son heads over to Cat and I grin, nudging him with my shoulder.

"Karma, huh?" I tease and he flips me off.

"Maybe they'll get married and have babies!" Indie says, coming up to stand next to Mischa.

"Indie! You're not helping," he says, taking a drink of water as he goes back to keeping an eye on his kid.

Not a lot has changed for me in the past eighteen years. I'm still married to Edie. She's still the love of my life and the best thing that has ever happened to me. She works as a translator, although she takes far less jobs. She decided on one a month while Zeke was growing up and now that he's heading off to college in the fall, she's talked about maybe doing more but she doesn't need to.

Zeke gave each of us part of the company and we've all been working to grow it into an empire here in Pittsburgh. We opened up a second location further uptown and Mischa and I both help to run that one. His son has been talking about apprenticing there and I know that we would all love to keep the business in the family. Sam and Max's daughter, Cat, has already started training under her mom and I have a feeling that we'll be handing it down to them. Maybe they really will get married and take over everything for us.

Edie and I decided that one kid was enough for us. The birth had been hard and I had hated seeing her in so much pain. She had Zeke and had taken one look at him before she turned to me and said we should name him Zeke Mischa Mitchell. She told me that she had always liked the idea of naming the baby after their grandpa but since her dad was a deadbeat and mine was well, mine, she thought we should name him after Zeke. She told me without them helping her, she didn't know if she would have gotten here so Zeke Mischa Mitchell it was. Mischa had laughed so hard at the grandpa part but Zeke and I had both been touched.

Edie's mom, Susan, had retired a few years ago and we built a little apartment in the basement of our place. That way she was there to help out with Zeke but she also got to spend more time with her daughter.

"Okay, dad," Zeke says as he comes over to me.

"Be respectful," I warn him as I pass him my keys.

"Duh," he says with a roll of his eyes but he's grinning and I pull him into a hug.

Mischa sees this and makes a beeline for the door but Max and Zeke catch him and drag him back.

"Group hug!" Sam yells and everyone laughs as Mischa tries to wiggle away.

I wrap my arms around Zeke and Edie and grin as I look out over this completely dysfunctional, crazy, totally perfect family that I found.

ABOUT THE AUTHOR

CONNECT WITH ME!

If you enjoyed this story, please consider leaving a review on Amazon or any other reader site or blog that you like. Don't forget to recommend it to your other reader friends.

If you want to chat with me, please consider joining my VIP list or connecting with me on one of my Social Media platforms. I love talking with each of my readers. Links below!

VIP list

ALSO BY SHAW HART

Remembering Valentine's Day

Finding Their Rhythm

Her Scottish Savior

Stealing Her

Hop Stuff

Dream Boat

Series by Shaw Hart

Telltale Heart Series

Bought and Paid For

His Miracle

Pretty Girl

Ash Mountain Pack Series

Growling For My Mate

Claiming My Mate

Mated For Life

Chasing My Mate

Protecting Our Mate

Love Note Series

Signing Off With Love

Care Package Love

Wrong Number, Right Love

Folklore Series

Kidnapped by Bigfoot

Loved by Yeti

Claimed by Her Sasquatch

Rescued by His Mermaid

Eye Candy Ink Series

Atlas

Mischa

Sam

Printed in Great Britain
by Amazon

79240067R00051